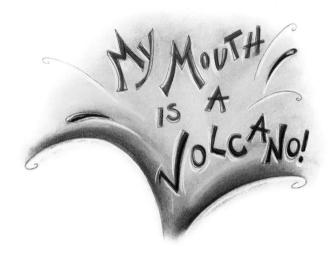

To Blanche, for giving me the gift of her time.

# Duplication and Copyright

Summary:
This book teaches children to manage their thoughts and words without interrupting.

P.O. Box 22185
Chattanooga, TN 37422-2185
423.899.5714 • 866.318.6294
fax: 423.899.4547
www.ncyi.org

ISBN: 978-1-931636-85-8    $9.95
© 2005 National Center for Youth Issues, Chattanooga, TN
All rights reserved.

Written by: Julia Cook
Illustrations by: Carrie Hartman
Published by National Center for Youth Issues
Softcover

Printed at RR Donnelley • Reynosa, Tamaulipas, Mexico • March 2018

My name is Louis. People say I erupt a lot. I don't think I do...I have a lot to say, and all of my words are very important to me.

When other people talk, words just pop into my head. Then they slide down onto my tongue.

My tummy starts to *rumble*, and then it starts to *grumble*.

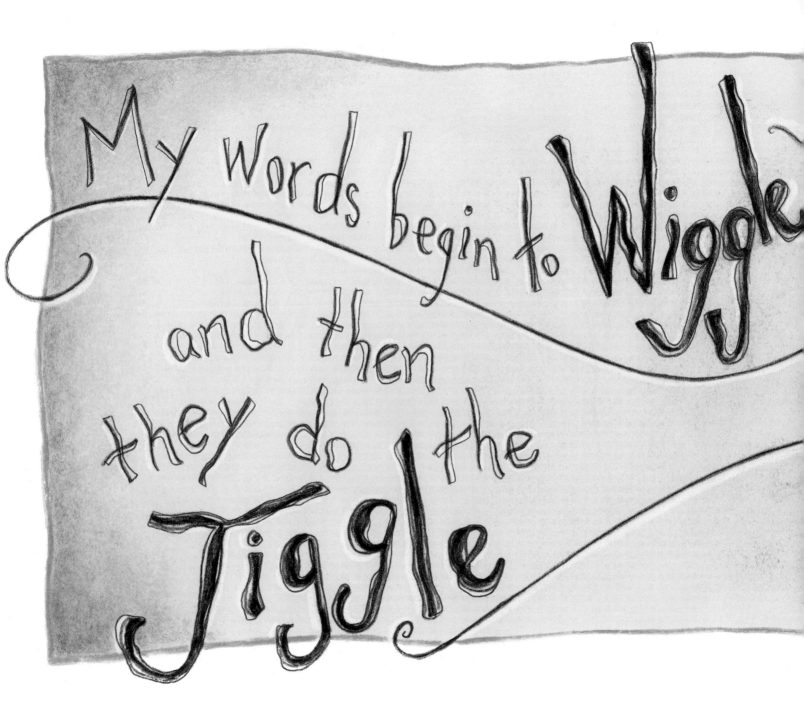

My words begin to Wiggle and then they do the Jiggle

My tongue pushes all of my important words up against my teeth, and then...

I Erupt!
Words just explode out of my mouth. My mouth is a volcano!!!

In class, my teacher says that when we want to say something, we are supposed to look at her, raise our hand, and wait until she calls on us. I tried that. After I waited patiently for what seemed like 62 years, my important words slid down from my head onto my tongue.

My tummy started to rumble, and then it started to grumble. My words began to wiggle, and then they did the jiggle. My tongue pushed all of my important words into my teeth and my volcano erupted!

My teacher was less than pleased. She erupted me right back! "I know what you are saying is very important to you, Louis, but since it is not an emergency, you'll have to wait until I call on you."

It was my volcano's fault.

At day care, we were sitting on the rug, listening to Miss Polly read us a story about planting trees. All of a sudden I thought about the time my grandpa and I planted six trees in his front yard!

My important words slid down from my head onto my tongue. My tummy started to rumble, and then it started to grumble. My words began to wiggle, and then they did the jiggle. My tongue pushed all of my important words into my teeth and my volcano erupted!

I got a time out.

It was my volcano's fault.

During dinner, Mom and Dad were talking about paying the bills. Then I thought about my friend Bill. Bill can blow a bubble inside of a bubble when he chews 2 pieces of bubble gum. Now that is *really* important!! My important words about Bill slid down from my head onto my tongue.

My tummy started to *rumble*, and then it started to *grumble*. My words began to *wiggle*, and then they did the *jiggle*. My tongue pushed all of my very important words into my teeth and my volcano erupted!

"Louis!" my mom said. "You interrupted AGAIN! If somebody else is talking, and you don't have an emergency, you have to wait for your tur...."

"But Mom! My words...they slide down from my head onto my tongue, then my tummy starts to rum...."

"Louis, you did it again!!!"

I got sent to my room. She said I was rude.

It was my volcano's fault!

The next day at school was my very important day.
I had been waiting for about 126 weeks to be the
"Student Star" of my class. This was 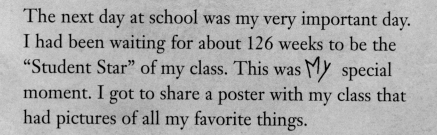 special
moment. I got to share a poster with my class that
had pictures of all my favorite things.

I stood up in front of my class and began to tell them about the time I went fishing.

Halfway through my story, Richard started to tell everyone about when he went deep-sea fishing in Mexico. His story must have been better than mine because everyone started to look at him. He was stealing my important words!!!!

"Richard," said my teacher, "you just interrupted Louis. Please wait until he is finished talking, and then he might call on you."
I couldn't believe how rude that was of Richard. He erupted ME! That REALLY made me angry.

After talking about my fishing trip, I started to explain the x-ray of my broken arm.
Just as I was getting to the good part, Courtney started to tell the class about when she
broke her leg.

"Courtney," said my teacher, "you just interrupted Louis. Please wait until he is finished talking, and then he might call on you."

I couldn't believe how rude that was of Courtney. She started talking right during my fifteen minutes of fame! She ruined my important words. She almost stole my moment.

25

When I got home, I told my mom about Rude Richard and Rude Courtney.

"Now you know how we feel when you interrupt us," said my mom.

"I never thought about that."

"I just get so excited and my words, they just pop into my head. Then they slide down onto my tongue. My tummy starts to rumble, and then it starts to grumble. My words begin to wiggle, and then they do the jiggle. Then, my tongue pushes all of my important words up against my teeth, and I erupt! Words just explode out of my mouth. My mouth is a volcano!!!"

"Maybe Richard and Courtney have volcanoes in their mouths, too," my mom replied.

"I never thought about that."

"Well, son, the next time your 'important words' are pushed into your teeth by your tongue, bite down hard and don't let them out. Then take a deep breath and push your words out through your nose. Then when it is your turn to talk, take a deep breath and breathe them back into your mouth."

"Will that work?" I asked.

"Only if you make it work," said my mom.

That night at the dinner table, my sister Sylvia was in the middle of one of her LONG "girl" stories, when my important words began to slide down from my head and my volcano started to do its thing. Just as my tongue started to push my words out through my teeth, I bit down really hard. Then I breathed my words out through my nose.

As soon as my sister finished talking, I took a deep breath, and back in went the words. I was amazed that they had just hung around outside my mouth and didn't float away.

Then I told my story, and nobody got mad at me for erupting.

After that, I never erupted again...well, except for the
time Bill's bubble gum got stuck in my hair.
But that was a REAL emergency!